SPY KIDS 2
THE ISLAND OF LOST DREAMS

Based on the screenplay by
Robert Rodriguez

Adapted by
Lara Bergen

talk miramax books

HYPERION BOOKS FOR CHILDREN
NEW YORK

Text © 2002 by Miramax Film Corp.
Story, art, and photographs © 2002 by Miramax Film Corp.

SPY kids™ is a trademark and the exclusive property of Miramax Film Corp. under license from Dimension Films, a division of Miramax Film Corp.
All Rights Reserved.

Cover photograph by Rico Torres

Photo credits: Rico Torres

Printed in the United States of America
First Edition
1 3 5 7 9 10 8 6 4 2

ISBN: 0-7868-1726-7
Library of Congress Catalog Card Number: 2002103714

Alexandra, the eleven-year-old daughter of the president of the United States, was at Troublemaker Studios Theme Park, surrounded by mascots and a TV crew. She was there to try out the new ride, the Juggler.

After the interview, Alexandra went on the ride and stood high at the top of the Juggler, refusing to come down. She held in her hand the nation's most top-secret device called the Transmooker. Both Alexandra and the Transmooker had to be saved, and only the OSS's two smallest and bravest agents could do it.

Juni and Carmen Cortez spun around to see the action. This was a job for experienced Spy Kids! But their competition, Gary and Gerti Giggles, stepped in and tried to steal their assignment.

Even though it was Carmen and Juni who saved the Transmooker device and the president's daughter, Gary and Gerti Giggles got all the credit. Later that night, the president and his daughter hosted an OSS banquet for international Spy Kids (and some grown-ups). Carmen and Juni saw the rival spies and their father, Donnagon Giggles, who was the new head of the OSS.

At first, Carmen and Juni had fun. Juni had some great moves on the dance floor!

But the next thing the Spy Kids knew, all the grown-ups in the room fell forward with a *THUNK* onto their dinner plates.

"Sleepers," said Carmen, sniffing her dad's champagne.

At the same time, every waiter in the room dropped his tray and began running toward the sleeping guest of honor—the president—and the Transmooker device.

Instantly, all the Spy Kids sprang into action. Together they charged at the phony waiters.

Juni went for the crook who had grabbed the Transmooker device—and so did Gary Giggles. At first, the two of them fought together. Gary knocked the man off his feet, while Juni pinned him down and snatched the device. Then Juni felt the Transmooker slip out of his hand. Gary had grabbed it—again!

"Give me that!" Juni yelled, lunging after Gary.

But before Juni could get it back, the Transmooker slid across the floor, away from both Gary and Juni, and right into the evil villain's hands.

The man smiled as he held the device up and pushed the red button. Suddenly, the lights in the banquet room dimmed, and every spy gadget in the room fell powerless to the ground.

Carmen's eyes scoured the room for another kind of weapon. Aha! she thought, grabbing a handful of spoons off a table. She began to fling them at the waiter.

"Ow!" he cried as the utensils clanged and banged off his metal helmet.

But just when Carmen thought she had him, the hall began to rumble and the spoons rose out of her hands. Not only that, but everything else metal in the room—including the crooks in their metal hats—began to float up toward a ship hovering just over the banquet hall's roof.

Within seconds, the magnet ship, the crooks, *and* the Transmooker were gone.

By early the next morning, the adults had awakened and Gary Giggles had blamed the whole robbery on Juni.

"I've been fired," Juni told his sister, back home in their tree house.

"I know," Carmen said. "I hacked into the OSS data files and saw the news."

But that wasn't all Carmen was able to do. She pressed a few more buttons on her workstation and grinned. She was in the OSS Agency's Top Secret Files.

And within a few minutes, Juni had his job back—complete with his own Level One status.

Carmen and Juni shared a high five. The Cortez kids were back in business!

The first thing they did was eavesdrop on Gary and Gerti's OSS briefing—with the help of Carmen's hacking skills and Juni's robot bug, RALPH.

"There is an area off the coast of Madagascar," Donnagon was saying to Gary and Gerti, "where boats have been disappearing for more than a year. Survivors tell tales of a mysterious island full of strange creatures. And the magnet ship that captured the Transmooker was last tracked in the same area. So . . . we need a small ship, piloted by two small agents, to get a closer look. This," he told Gary and Gerti, "is the Ukata assignment."

"We accept," Gary and Gerti replied.

"You bet we accept," said Carmen. And she began to type some more.

Carmen had just finished programming in a new job for Gary and Gerti and reassigning the Ukata mission to herself and Juni, when an unexpected visitor arrived. Quickly, the duo scaled the wall to the ceiling.

"I've brought you the very latest in gadgets and spy gear," Uncle Machete said. He knew right away to look up above to find his niece and nephew.

"Good," said Carmen, "'cause we're gonna need it."

Machete showed them the very latest spy watch—complete with cell phone, Internet access,

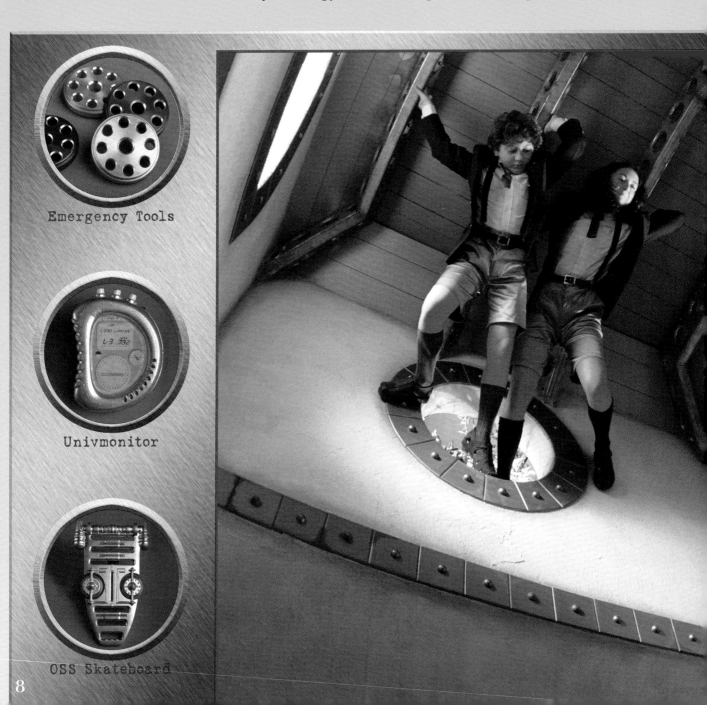

Emergency Tools

Univmonitor

OSS Skateboard

and satellite TV. Then he gave them the one gadget he said that they should always carry.

"A rubber band?" Carmen asked.

"A Machete Elastic Wonder," Machete corrected. "Nine hundred ninety-nine uses. And the best thing is that you have to figure out what they are. Just remember, you still need to be self-sufficient. That's something no gadget in the world can ever replace."

Then it was off to the OSS's underground parking lot. Carmen and Juni were ready for the mission.

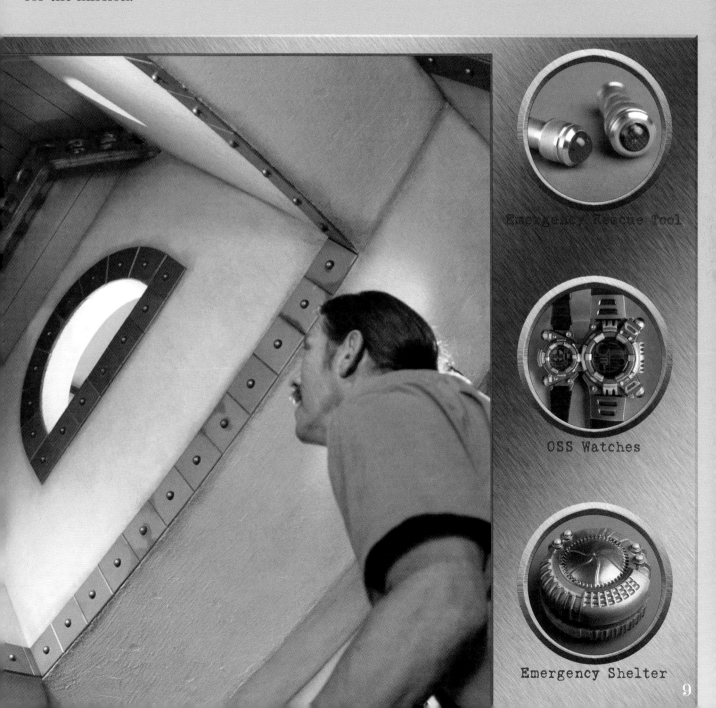

Emergency Rescue Tool

OSS Watches

Emergency Shelter

"WELCOME TO THE *DragonSpy*," the sub's computer announced as Carmen and Juni climbed in.

Carmen tapped into the OSS's Ukata files, hoping to find out more information. But instead she found something even stranger: photos of Donnagon and a mysterious man studying what looked like the president's Transmooker.

"There's only one person I know who can help us with these secrets," Carmen said. That's when she picked up the phone and dialed Minion's number.

"What do you make of this?" she asked the man who had once been the Spy Kids' enemy but had since joined them to fight evil.

Minion twitched his four noses. "Smells like the work of Donnagon Giggles," he said. "The man's dirt. Find the island," he instructed. "Then find the Island Man, Donnagon's contact."

Carmen thanked him and hung up just as the spy sub's computer told them they were nearing their destination zone. But then, all of a sudden, their spy ship began shaking. The computer shut down. And they started to sink.

"My flashlight won't even work!" Carmen said as they hurried toward the ship's gear room. Nothing electrical was working.

Carmen and Juni cracked open some glow sticks and grabbed two super inflate-a-suits.

"These should work," Carmen said. "They're valve-operated, not electrical in any way." And sure enough, the suits filled with air and shot them to the surface.

The two tried their best to paddle in their enormous rubber suits toward an island in the distance. They tried so hard, in fact, they never saw the giant sea monster rise up behind them, open its massive jaws, and move in for a bite. . . .

All they knew was that when its fangs hit the rubber, their suits sent them like giant balloons straight onto the island's rocky beach.

On the island, Carmen and Juni soon discovered that none of their fancy spy gadgets could help them make camp or contact home. They had to try to start a fire with a stick!

"Maybe it's the island," said Carmen—"some sort of cloaking device with a force strong enough to remove the place from radar and disable our equipment. . . ."

"No gadgets?!" cried Juni. "You mean we're gonna have to use our heads?"

Juni and Carmen explored the island, climbing up a volcano until they reached the top. "Get away from the edge!" Carmen warned her brother.

But it was too late. The rocks beneath Juni rumbled, and he fell headfirst into the mouth of the volcano. Carmen tried to catch him, but she failed and plunged downward, too.

Down, down, down they fell, for what seemed to them like hours. Until at last—with a gut-wrenching *WHOMP!*—they came to a sudden stop.

Slowly, Carmen and Juni opened their eyes to find themselves hovering just inches above a miniature model of the island volcano—blasting enough air to keep them from landing.

Suddenly, a mysterious figure stepped out from behind a pillar. Was this . . . the Island Man?

"I'm . . . Romero," he said slowly. "Sole inhabitant of this island . . . of . . . Leeke Leeke. Sole . . . *human* . . . inhabitant, that is." Then he flipped a switch, and the Spy Kids dropped to the floor.

Romero led Carmen and Juni into a dusty old lab, where he showed them a tiny cage filled with real, live, tiny animals—the scientist wanted to create a miniature zoo so kids could have their own small animals.

"But then," Romero went on, "one day I accidentally mixed up two test tubes and created new species altogether. . . ."

Romero showed them another cage filled with crazy, combined animals—half horses, half flies; half cats, half fish; half lizards, half snakes. . . .

"Then," the inventor finally explained, "I began to think . . . if only I could make them a wee bit bigger. . . . So I applied growth serum . . . and that's where things went . . . very wrong."

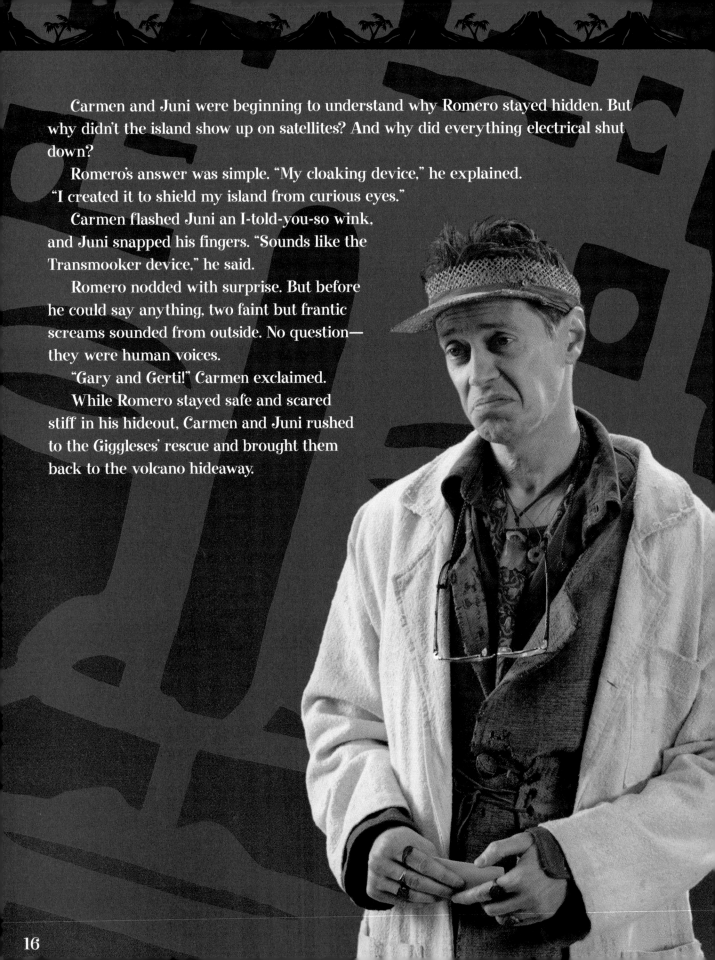

Carmen and Juni were beginning to understand why Romero stayed hidden. But why didn't the island show up on satellites? And why did everything electrical shut down?

Romero's answer was simple. "My cloaking device," he explained. "I created it to shield my island from curious eyes."

Carmen flashed Juni an I-told-you-so wink, and Juni snapped his fingers. "Sounds like the Transmooker device," he said.

Romero nodded with surprise. But before he could say anything, two faint but frantic screams sounded from outside. No question— they were human voices.

"Gary and Gerti!" Carmen exclaimed.

While Romero stayed safe and scared stiff in his hideout, Carmen and Juni rushed to the Giggleses' rescue and brought them back to the volcano hideaway.

"Relax," Carmen told Romero, who was peeking out from under a table. "They're OSS agents as well."

"OSS?" Romero said, perking up.

Juni stared at him suspiciously. "You work for the OSS, don't you?" he said.

Romero nodded. "I work for a man named Donnagon."

All of a sudden, things made sense to Carmen and Juni. "Donnagon hired you to make these creatures, didn't he?" Carmen said. "Or so he told you. But what he really wants is your cloaking device—the Transmooker!"

"And now that Donnagon's head of the OSS," Juni went on, "he has the power to take it from you."

The device stolen from the president was just a prototype. What Donnagon truly wanted was the one on this very island—one powerful enough to shut down technology throughout the entire planet.

In the wrong hands, the Transmooker device could end the world as Juni and Carmen knew it. There was just one thing to do: destroy the Transmooker now. But how?

"Where is the Transmooker?" Carmen demanded.

Romero pointed to a high peak on the other side of the island. "It's not easy to get to," he warned them. "The journey alone is more dangerous than the Transmooker itself."

But danger had never stopped Carmen and Juni before. They jumped into Romero's magnetically powered hovercraft and set off.

Meanwhile, Carmen and Juni's parents had got the news from Donnagon: the two Spy Kids sent on the Ukata assignment were lost . . . and those two Spy Kids were Carmen and Juni! Now, not only were their parents looking for them—but so were their grandparents.

Right away, the family readied their giant spy sub for a rescue and set off. And thanks to some nonelectrical tracking devices Gregorio had planted in Carmen's and Juni's teeth, their parents and grandparents were soon able to pinpoint their destination and were hot on their trail.

As soon as they thought they were safe, Carmen and Juni stopped to catch their breath and check their location. As Juni studied the map Romero had given them, he pulled a freeze-dried spy snack out of his pocket and took a bite. *Mmmm*, he sighed. He hadn't eaten all day, and his stomach sure was rumbling . . .

. . . Or was it? Slowly, Juni turned around. *Agh!* That wasn't the sound of his stomach rumbling. That was the growl of a giant creature—half spider and half ape—creeping toward him on huge, gangly spider legs and letting out gruesome roars.

"Let's go now!" Carmen yelled.

Carmen spied a narrow gap in the rocks leading to an underwater cave. It was just big enough for her and Juni to squeeze through. And just small enough to keep huge mutant creatures away. . . .

Carmen stared at Juni, and Juni stared back.

Juni opened his mouth to say something, but nothing came out. Strangely, Carmen knew what her brother had wanted to say.

We can hear each other's thoughts! they both discovered at the same time.

Then Juni spotted a big gold medallion between two skeletons. Cool! thought Juni.

Put it back, Juni! Carmen warned silently.

Juni thought about it a moment. Then, when Carmen had turned her back, he reached over and grabbed the medallion.

Uh-oh! Suddenly, Carmen and Juni found themselves at the edge of a rocky cliff, with dozens of angry, armed skeleton pirates just steps behind them. The skeletons had come alive!

Carmen roundhouse-kicked the closest one and shattered him into a million pieces. Then she quickly took his armor. But no sooner had the skeleton fallen apart than it put itself back together again and started charging once more.

"We're doomed!" Carmen moaned. But just as she was about to yell at Juni for swiping the medallion, a loud *SCREECH!* pierced the air, and one of Romero's creatures, a giant spork, dove down and plucked Carmen off the ledge.

"Carmen!" Juni cried. But how was he going to rescue her when the skeleton he had robbed was charging at him with a rusty sword held high?

Juni closed his eyes and held up the medallion, preparing himself for the worst. *WHOOSH!*

Slowly, Juni opened his eyes. The skeleton had grabbed the medallion back. But instead of cutting off Juni's head, the skeleton had flipped the sword around and was offering the handle to Juni.

"Thanks, Bones!" Juni said. And sword in hand, he set off to find his sister.

"CARRRR . . . MEN!" Juni called out for the hundredth time as he scaled down the mountain. He pulled out his freeze-dried snack again and wearily opened his mouth to take a bite.

ROOAAARRR!

All of a sudden, a giant spider-ape was standing over him and drooling. Juni looked back and forth between the beast and his snack bar. Wait a minute, he thought to himself. Was the spider-ape just hungry?

"You like honey-roasted ham and potatoes?" Juni asked, offering his bar up to the creature.

Sure enough, the spider-ape gobbled it up within seconds.

But Juni's problems were far from over. While he was making friends with the spider-ape, Gary Giggles had tamed another creature, the slizzard, with his own freeze-dried snack and was now riding its scaly back—straight up to Juni.

It was a fierce and furious battle between Spy Kids and monster creatures.

"Take that!" Juni cried as the spider-ape pounced on the slizzard and sent it flying into a rock wall. But the slizzard crawled back up and wrapped its neck around a tall stone column. Then, with a mighty tug, it sent the pillar crashing down on both the spider-ape and Juni.

"It's all over for you, squirt," Gary sneered as his slizzard loomed, hissing over Juni.

Juni tried to stand tall. But was this the end . . . ?

Then, all of a sudden, something leaped down from the trees and knocked Gary off his slizzard. It was Carmen! She had escaped from the giant spork's nest—along with Gerti Giggles.

"Don't mess with me!" Carmen warned both Gary and the scaly creature. Then she turned to her brother. "We have to destroy the Transmooker device *now!*" she said.

Together the two helped pull the spider-ape to its feet. Then they climbed on its back and sped away. At last they reached an ancient temple built high on a steep, funnel-shaped mountain. Inside they found an enormous and powerful-looking machine: the Transmooker device!

"Is that it?" Juni asked.

"Yes," Carmen nodded.

"How do you know?"

"'Cause it's big and weird and in the middle of the room."

"Good point," said Juni. Then he reached out and gently touched it.

Juni studied the instructions Romero had sent with them. Then he looked at the Transmooker more closely.

"There should be five safety switches," he told Carmen. "One, two, three, four . . ."

Just then, the door flew open, and in raced Gary and Gerti, Romero . . . and Donnagon!

"Five," Juni said as he flipped the final switch—and the whole machine lit up.

"What did I do?" Juni cried.

"You started it!" cried Romero.

And then it happened. The whole world stopped!

"What do we do?" Juni asked Romero.

"You must bind the five toggle switches together," Romero called out.

But how? Juni wondered. Then he got an idea. He grabbed the Machete Elastic Wonder out of Carmen's hair and swiftly stretched it around all five switches. Within seconds, lights all over the planet came back on, and the world was up and running again.

Still, Carmen knew the danger wasn't over yet. Thinking quickly, she hit another switch and lifted a heavy metal piece out of the Transmooker. It was just like the president's prototype, but ten times bigger.

"Give it to me!" Donnagon yelled, lunging for Carmen.

But Carmen wasn't about to let the device fall into Donnagon's evil hands. She threw it to Romero, who immediately tossed it out the window . . . and into the talons of a spork gliding by.

Gerti stole a glance at Carmen, then took a step forward. "I know where the spork's nest is, Dad," she told her father.

And soon another chase was under way.

Now that the Transmooker was turned off, Carmen and Juni's spy gadgets were working again. Carmen and Juni had a new means of transportation—their rocket shoes! They blasted past the Giggleses and snatched the Transmooker out of the spork's nest, this time using their Elastic Wonder as a giant slingshot.

"An agent's only as good as her gadgets!" Carmen taunted Gary and Gerti and their dad.

Then Carmen and Juni raced back to the beach . . . where to their surprise they found their parents and grandparents waiting to see them! Then Donnagon appeared with the Transmooker prototype in hand and a cruel smile on his face.

"It couldn't be any more perfect," he said. He had the *whole* Cortez family just where he wanted them—just as he had planned!

He aimed the device at the group, shutting down their sub and gadgets. Then he took the real Transmooker from Carmen and handed it to Gerti.

"Reprogram it," he ordered her. "I want to start by erasing the Cortez family from the face of the earth."

Gerti worked on the Transmooker, then gave it back to her father. Donnagon grinned cruelly. Then he raised the device, aimed it, pressed the red button, and—

KABOOOM!

Instead of zapping the Cortezes, the Transmooker suddenly exploded in Donnagon's hands.

"Gerti . . . What did you . . . ? Why?" he asked, bewildered.

"Don't even get me started," Gerti said, shaking her head. "Just wait till Mom finds out you tried to take over the world—again!"

While Romero's creatures gathered peacefully around him, an armada of black presidential chopper cars swooped down upon the beach. Out stepped the president and his smiling daughter.

"By order of the president," the president's daughter said, walking up to Gary, "you've been disavowed." Then she removed his Level One badge and handed it to Juni.

As the island below their chopper faded out of view, Juni hugged his parents. Then he looked down at the thank-you present from Romero in his lap. Slowly, he lifted the lid of the box . . . and he grinned at the sight of the miniature spider-ape climbing up inside.

Carmen and Juni smiled. Mission accomplished!